# THE SUNDAY BLUES

A book for school children, school teachers, and anybody else who dreads Monday mornings.

HODDER CHILDREN'S BOOKS

First published in Great Britain in 2002 by Hodder and Stoughton
This edition first published in 2020

Text and illustrations copyright © Neal Layton 2002

The moral rights of the author have been asserted.

A CIP catalogue record for this book is
available from the British Library.

ISBN: 978 1 44495 562 0

1 3 5 7 9 10 8 6 4 2

Printed and bound in China

FSC
www.fsc.org

MIX
Paper from
responsible sources
FSC® C104740

Hodder Children's Books
An imprint of Hachette Children's Group
Part of Hodder and Stoughton
Carmelite House, 50 Victoria Embankment,
London, EC4Y 0DZ

An Hachette UK Company
www.hachette.co.uk
www.hachettechildrens.co.uk

# THE SUNDAY BLUES

Written and illustrated by

*Neal Layton*

Hodder
Children's
Books

It was Sunday and Steve was fed up.

He was fed up because it was Sunday and because that meant tomorrow was Monday and because that meant SCHOOL!

"Why don't we pop in on Auntie Vera on the way back?" suggested Steve's mum.

Going home, Steve became really sad
because it was school the next day,
and he would miss Benny
and Mum and Dad . . .

. . . and he was sure to have a terrible day there,
because school was really, really, really horrible.

After his bath, Steve's dad read a really exciting story about pirates.

# That night, Steve had lots of dreams . . .

. . . and then he woke up.

The moment he had been dreading all Sunday had finally arrived. It was time for school.

At the gates, Steve could see his school friends in the playground, waiting for the bell to call them to lessons.

Steve said goodbye to his mum and joined his friends in the playground.

Perhaps school wouldn't be so bad after all!